# How to Stop Armadillo Tears

By Mark Bowles, Ph.D.
Juanita Gandara, M.Ed.

Illustrated by Christopher Dart

ISBN 9781650232812 First Edition

Dedication from Mark:

I would like to dedicate this book to my mother. She was my first reader, writing down stories that I told her before I learned to write in school. A half century later I am still learning to write, and I thank my mother for remaining an enthusiastic reader.

Dedication from Juanita:

In memory of my loving parents (Natalia Quinones Soto & Prudenciano "Chano" Quinones) and to all my family (including Margarita Reyes Hernandez), friends, educators, students, parents and communities who crossed my path and whom I was fortunate enough to serve and get to know.  Thank you for always allowing me to feel that I was "Blessed to be a blessing!"

**On a sunny Texas morning,**
**Armando the armadillo**
**approaches a pack of dogs on a school playground...**

Hello, my name is Armando,
And guess what?
I am a special armadillo!

I am new here today,
And I am looking for someone
Who might like to play.

Hi! I am Eduardo the Encyclopedia, and I want to share fun facts about this story and also ask questions so I can get to know you! I am "bilingual," which means I speak two languages. I know English and Spanish. Do you know any words in Spanish?

**One of the dogs turns to say...**

We already have friends
And have no room for more.
Besides, you seem strange.
Are you a lost dinosaur?

You have a shell,
Which is so hard and thick.
How old are you?
Are you prehistoric?

ENCYCLOPEDIA

The time before humans is known as "prehistoric/prehistórico,"
and that is when dinosaurs roamed the earth.
Have you ever seen a dinosaur in a museum?

**Despite his rugged appearance,**
**Armando's feelings are hurt. He responds...**

I am not a dinosaur!
Do I look big and mean?
I don't stomp around,
Or roar and scream.

I am a mammal
Just like you.
I love music, country dancing,
And singing too.

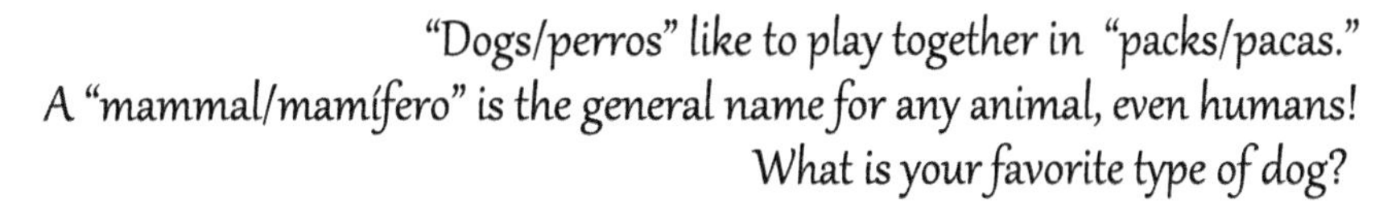

*"Dogs/perros" like to play together in "packs/pacas."*
*A "mammal/mamífero" is the general name for any animal, even humans!*
*What is your favorite type of dog?*

**The dogs think that the idea of a musical armadillo is funny...**

An armadillo that sings?
You hear that, hounds?
Can you imagine
such silly sounds?

We dogs are musical,
Barking all night and day.
We love to howl our songs...
Ruff! Ruff!... in our canine way!

A "canine/canino" is another word for a dog!
Do you have a pet canine, or another animal at home? What is it?

**The pack of dogs dash away from Armando, and he thinks to himself...**

I wish those dogs knew that I make music too.
They could tap, tap, tap on my shell,
Playing me like a bongo to
Keep the tempo so well!

Or I could even become
An instrument to strum.
Armadillos make music both ways,
With strings or a drum.

But the dogs will never know.

A "Charango" is a stringed lute instrument that looks like a small guitar. They are often made from armadillo shells. It has the same name in English and Spanish! Do you play an instrument?

**Armando walks towards a clowder of cats swinging on the school playground...**

Hello, my name is Armando,
And guess what?
I am a special armadillo!

I would love to play,
But those dogs said,
"Ruff! Ruff! ... No way, Jose!"

"A clowder of cats" means a "group of cats." In Spanish you would say, "un polvo de gatos." Have you ever seen a cat play with a ball of yarn? What is your favorite toy?

**The cats hunch their backs and roll their eyes...**

We never agree with those dogs,
But for once they speak true.
Who would want to play
With a creature like you?

Let me tell you a joke.
What is the opposite of a soft pillow?
Everyone knows...
Meow! Meow!... It is an armadillo!

*In English cats "meow," and in Spanish they "maullar."*
*What color of cat do you like the best?*

**Another cat snickers and says...**

You are not like us!<br>
We are furry, soft, and clean.<br>
We walk around our alleys<br>
Like proud kings and queens.

You are hard as a rock<br>
And truth be told,<br>
If you were in a pet store,<br>
You would never be sold!

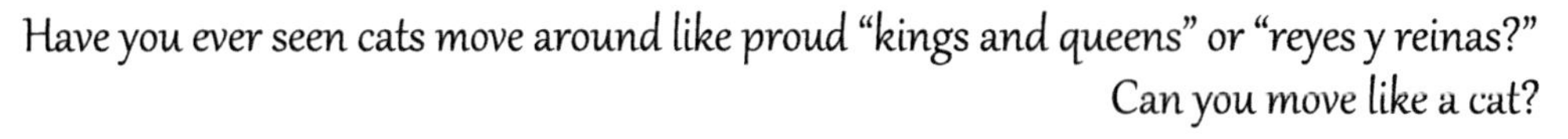

*Have you ever seen cats move around like proud "kings and queens" or "reyes y reinas?"*
*Can you move like a cat?*

**As the cats prance away, Armando grows sadder...**

I wish those cats knew
I once had soft skin.
Then as I began to grow,
My awesome armor came in!

Even now, my tummy
Is covered with fur,
And as a baby,
I could even purr!

But the cats will never know.

In English, cats "purr" when they are happy and in Spanish they "ronronean."
What sound do you make when you are happy? I like to giggle!

**Armando walks alone and looking up, sees a parliament of owls in a tree...**

Hello, my name is Armando,
And guess what?
I am a special armadillo!

I would love to play,
But the dogs and cats said,
"Ruff, Meow... Not today!"

*A group of "owls/búhos" is known as "a parliament/un parlamento."*
*If you could fly like an owl, where would you go?*

**One owl slowly opens his eyes and turns his head around and then down...**

Do not be such a bother,
For we are owls in trees,
Who prefer our time alone,
Without play buddies.

You cannot teach us,
For we are wise you see,
Now, let us study...
Hoot! Hoot!... Leave us be.

*"Owls Hoot," while "Buhos Bramean."*
*An owl can see all the way around its body,*
*just by turning its head.*
*How far can you look to the left and right?*

**The owls fly away, and Armando's eyes start to water...**

If the owls had not flown,
I could have taught them something
They had never known.

The number of bands on our shells
Is one way to know our names.
There are so many types of us,
You can make it a guessing game!

But the owls will never know.

A "pink fairy armadillo" in Spanish is called an "armadillo de una hada rosa" and is identified by 24 bands around its shell. How do you recognize people you meet?

**Armando walks to the edge of the playground to a sleuth of bears fishing by a stream...**

Hello, my name is Armando,
And guess what?
I am a special armadillo!

I would love to play, but the
Dogs, cats, and owls said,
"Ruff, Meow, Hoot.... go away!"

*In English, a "group of bears" is called a "sleuth." In Spanish, they are referred to as "Un grupo de osos." What is your favorite type of bear? A brown, black, panda, or polar bear?*

**The bears look grumpy because their tummies are growling...**

We bears are hungry<br>
And need something to eat.<br>
We are trying to catch fish<br>
For our afternoon treat.

What could an armadillo do?<br>
Hey cubs, what do you think?<br>
If we threw him in the water...<br>
Growl, Growl!... He would just sink.

*A "cub/cachorro" is a baby bear. They all like to "growl/gruñir."*
*What noise does your tummy make when you are hungry? Do you get grumpy?*

**The bears walk further up the stream.**
**With glistening eyes, Armando dreams...**

If only I had a wish,
I could have helped the bears fish.

Armadillos can hold their breath
A very, very long time.
Just imagine the food
I could help the bears find.

And we don't sink.
We swallow air and float,
Sometimes walking under the water,
Or swimming along like a boat.

But the bears will never know.

*Next time you are in a pool, try to "swim like an armadillo," or "nadar como un armadillo."*
*Do you know how to swim?*

**Armando turns away from the stream and finds a colony of bouncing bunnies playing hopscotch...**

Hello, my name is Armando,
And guess what?
I am a special armadillo!

I would love to play with you and run.
But the dogs, cats, owls, and bears said,
"Ruff, Meow, Hoot, Growl… you're no fun."

A group of "rabbits/conejos" is a "colony/colonia."
Do you have a name for your group of friends?

**The rabbits stop their hopping to consider, then giggle...**

You look like a turtle,
Walking with a shell so slow.
Who ever heard
of a running armadillo?

Bunnies are the best
Because of our great speed,
Now watch out as we...
Purr! Purr!... Bound through the weeds.

*Rabbits make two sounds when they are happy: "purr/ronronean" or "cluck/cloquean." Maybe sometimes they think they are a cat or a chicken! Can you hop like a bunny?*

**Armando watches their bushy tails scamper away.**
**A tear descends his tiny face...**

I suppose I look slow,
But my legs can really go!

Some armadillos can even beat
A fast rabbit in a race.
I don't need to win,
I just like to scamper and chase.

Armadillos can run fast,
Up to 30 miles per hour!
Just because my legs are short
Does not mean they lack power.

But the rabbits will never know.

*"Armadillos can run fast," or "Los armadillos pueden correr rápido."*
*What do you think is the fastest animal? Cheetahs run 70 MPH!*

**After no animals will play,**
**Armando lets out a crying moan.**
**With giant armadillo tears streaming,**
**He feels completely alone.**

**Suddenly, he hears hooves,**
**Sees black and white, and**
**Watches a striped zebra**
**Come into sight.**

*"Black and white" in Spanish is "En blanco y negro." What is your favorite color?*

**This time, the zebra approaches the armadillo...**

Hello, my name is Zoila,<br>
And guess what?<br>
I am a special zebra!

When I see an animal<br>
Starting to cry,<br>
I walk right up<br>
And just say, "Hi!"

So, will you be my new armadillo friend? Will you play with me today?

*If you see someone is sad or lonely, one great thing to do is "Just say hi" or "Nada mas decir hola."*<br>
*What do you say or do when you meet someone new?*

**Armando is so happy to finally find a friend. He wipes his eyes and suggests some special ways armadillos can have fun.**

**First, they make music together, playing Armando's shell like a drum.**

**Until the dogs return to visit...**

Ruff! Ruff!
Armando, you make great sounds
With those cool drum beats,
And if we added that to our singing,
It would be such a musical treat.

Tomorrow when we come back, will you join our pack?

Zoila loves to "dance/bailar" to country music, cumbias, and corridas.
Do you like to dance? What is your best move?

**Armando begins to smile a little and says, "Yes, thank you!" Next, the armadillo shows Zoila his shell and soft tummy.**

**Until the cats return...**

Meow! Meow!
Armando, we wish we had a shell
To make us tough as a log.
We would never have to run and hide
From those silly dogs!

Nothing would make us prouder. Would you would join our clowder?

*There is a saying, "Sticks and stones may break my bones, but words can never hurt me!" But words and actions CAN hurt. What can you do for someone who is sad because words or actions have hurt them?*

**Armando purrs sounds of happiness to the surprised cats. Then he begins to teach Zoila more about armadillos.**

**Until the owls fly over...**

Hoot! Hoot!
How fascinating to learn
About your breed.
You have many talents,
knowledge, and speed.

Astonishment! Would you come and teach in our owl parliament?

*Everyone has hidden "talents/talentos." It is fun to discover new ones in people! What is one of your hidden talents?*

**Armando stands wisely with a growing smile.**
**Next, he leads Zoila to a stream to swim.**

**Until the bears waddle over...**

Growl! Growl!
With those water skills,
We now ask you please,
Come fish with us tomorrow,
So we can all fill our bellies!

Tell us the truth, will you join our sleuth?

*To invite someone to play, just say "Join us!" or "Vamos a jugar!"*
*How would you invite someone to join your group?*

**Armando is so honored that the big bears want his help. Finally, he and Zoila decide to have a friendly chase.**

**Until the rabbits hop over excitedly...**

Purr! Purr!
We hardly believe our eyes,
Seeing such an amazing race!
WOW the zebra is fast,
But the armadillo kept his pace.

Tomorrow will you run in our bunny colony?

*A cat purrs with their throats, while a rabbit purrs by rubbing their "teeth" or "dientes" together! Would you rather run a race against a zebra, an armadillo, or a rabbit?*

**Finally, Armando smiles.**
**The sun sets and he is tired.**
**He thanks his new friend Zoila for coming to his rescue.**

**Before he goes home, he asks her...**

Why did you play
With me today,
When everyone else
Went away?

*This is VERY important in every language, "Everyone is special!" or "Todos somos especiales." Find someone you do not know very well and find out what is special about him or her! What was it?*

**Zoila is wise and knows everyone is special!**

**She shares her Words of Wisdom...**

If the pack of dogs,
Clowder of cats,
Parliament of owls,
Sleuth of bears,
And colony of rabbits
All welcomed a stranger today,
They could have had more fun
With new ways to play.

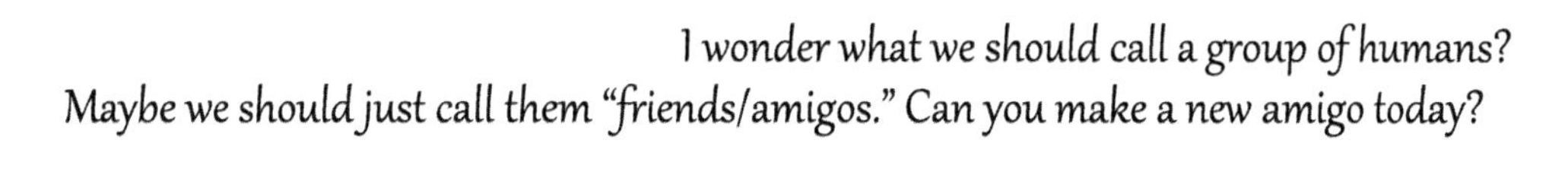

*I wonder what we should call a group of humans?*
*Maybe we should just call them "friends/amigos." Can you make a new amigo today?*

**Zoila puts her leg around Armando and smiles...**

Armando, please remember this:
Be your best self.
Don't be rude.
Be humble and kind.
Never exclude.

Slow or fast,
Be a friend to all.
Everyone is special,
Large or small.

And always use
Your eyes and ears,
To rescue anyone
With Armadillo tears.

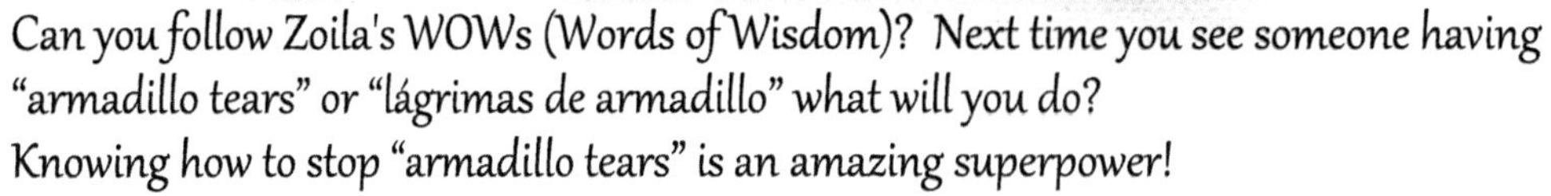

*Can you follow Zoila's WOWs (Words of Wisdom)? Next time you see someone having "armadillo tears" or "lágrimas de armadillo" what will you do?*
*Knowing how to stop "armadillo tears" is an amazing superpower!*

# The End

Made in the USA
Columbia, SC
20 January 2022

54532438R00020